I0538041

FOLLOWING FAITH

LONESOME HEARTS SERIES

JACQUI NELSON

Cover design by The Killion Group, Inc
ISBN ebook: 978-0-9936387-7-0
ISBN print: 978-0-9936387-6-3

DEDICATION

For Peggy Clayton for being an enthusiastic reader
and a wonderful friend.

You make an author want to keep writing.

CHAPTER 1

Oregon Territory
Autumn 1852

"You're relieved from your duties, Miss Featherby." Mr. Hammond tucked his bearded chin under his sagging collar, seeking respite from the squalls that tested Timber Creek's logging camp more days than not during Faith Featherby's three years teaching in the wilderness.

Although she habitually shied away from confrontations, this wasn't one she could accept mutely. "For how long? The children need me."

Hovering at the foot of the schoolhouse steps, Hammond's usually kind eyes remained downcast as he stared at Faith—or rather her feet, which were frozen in her bewilderment to the threshold of a structure that doubled as her lodgings.

"Your presence as Timber Creek's schoolmistress is no longer desirable," Hammond replied in a staccato voice, as if reciting from a script. Under eyebrows thick as woolly caterpillars, his eyes darted left then right, toward Mrs. Cain and Mrs. Crisp, who flanked him. "The school committee has voted. You're to leave immediately 'n never return."

An avalanche of fear hit Faith. She clutched the doorframe of the one-room shanty she'd transformed into a safe haven for her students and herself. Becoming a teacher had been her ticket out of the orphanage she'd grown up in. A ticket she'd hoped would lead to a better future.

"I've nowhere to go."

Mrs. Crisp's arctic-blue gaze chilled her to the bone. "You'll find room in a bawdy house."

"Jezebel," Mrs. Cain hissed under her breath.

"Whore of Babylon," Mrs. Crisp added, lightning-quick.

A gasp broke from Faith's lips before she could swallow it along with her hurt. From day one, the two women had mistaken her shyness for conceit and never uttered a kind word to her, or about her. But until today, they'd never gone so far as to slander her character.

Hammond raised his palms in a placating

manner, but his gaze dipped even lower, locking onto his own feet. "Ladies, please. Ain't no need for name callin'."

Mrs. Crisp sniffed in disdain. "She brought this on herself."

"What do you mean?" Faith slumped against the doorway and struggled to speak over her rising panic. "I've done nothing wrong."

Mrs. Cain's spindly body snapped straight as a pencil while her voice climbed high enough to make even Hammond flinch. "You consider relations outside marriage *nothing*?"

"Who said—?" An appalling notion pierced Faith.

Last week Dan Doolan had been furious when she rejected his overtures of *relations outside marriage*, which he'd proclaimed was her only prospect considering her advancing spinsterhood and lack of social graces. He'd preyed on her weaknesses. She could very well end up in a bawdy house—unable to elude men like Doolan—if she lost this job. She had few savings and no family or friends.

She forced herself to stand tall. "I have never participated in relations of those types."

Hammond's eyebrows bunched together as he frowned at the cut line where the woodsmen, including Doolan, labored unseen but still heard.

Their constant chopping and cussing filled the air from sunup to sundown.

"You're sayin' Doolan is lyin'?"

If she did not, she'd be branded a harlot. If she did, Doolan would soon be harassing her for slandering *his* name. "He's...not telling the truth." She cringed at the halting quaver in her voice.

Even though Mrs. Crisp stood below Faith, the woman managed to stare down her nose at her. "Mr. Doolan is a long upstanding member of this community."

"I've lived here as long as he has," Faith protested.

Mrs. Cain crossed her arms. "We know him. We do not know you."

Dan Doolan made himself *known* by intruding into people's lives.

Before Faith could round up the gumption to say so, Mrs. Crisp said, "Pegged her for a sinner from the start."

Mrs. Cain gave a curt nod. "Always suspected she was hiding something."

Faith's crippling shyness had prevented her from connecting with anyone in the camp, except for the children she taught. Children had curious minds. Adults often had theirs locked tight. But Mrs. Cain and Mrs. Crisp were right to sense Faith was hiding something. It just wasn't what they currently believed.

"You'd cast me into the wilderness with"—she gestured to the circle of trees, the lifeblood of this community, and the unknown beyond—"the wolves?"

"You'll fit right in with them," Mrs. Crisp replied. "And the savages, too. Only you would adopt a crow-bait Indian nag and squander your time nursing it back to health."

"The mare deserved a second chance." The sweet-tempered pinto had been ridden until winded and lame, and then discarded to limp into the camp seeking refuge. "Don't we all?"

Mrs. Cain's exaggerated scoff made her rock like a soaring Ponderosa Pine ready to come crashing down. "Not when our children are involved. Only a dullard such as you would suggest such a thing."

"Always questioned her intelligence."

"Probably lied about her credentials."

"We'll file a complaint so no one ever employs her again."

Mrs. Cain and Crisp's swift exchange left Faith's head spinning.

"No, we won't!" Hammond's voice rose along with his gaze until he finally looked Faith in the eye.

Hope flared in her heart and sprang forth in a

grateful smile. He wouldn't let them oust her from her home and livelihood. He'd help her.

He blinked as if dumbfounded, and more than a little bedazzled, by her smile. Hanging onto the suspenders bordering his heart, he burrowed his chin back under his collar. "Miss Featherby, I'm sorry, but the school committee's minds are set." He spun away from Faith and her condemners. Once his feet started moving, he gained speed and didn't stop. "You should get goin' before you make matters worse," he called over his shoulder. "God keep you safe on your journey."

CHAPTER 2

*W*ith Timber Creek behind her and the sun struggling to break through the morning mist ahead, Faith stared at the fork in the road. Sitting on Spirit, the mare she'd nursed from footsore to sprightly, she faced the first decision on her journey: take the main road or turn onto the narrow trail that led to Bird's Eye Pass.

Faith stroked Spirit's snowy mane, hoping to draw strength from the mare. Spirit would keep her safe as much as God would.

Even though Mrs. Cain and Mrs. Crisp ridiculed her for helping the mare, she'd never regret that decision. She slid the daguerreotype from the pocket that appeared custom-made for it in the simple riding blanket that served as Spirit's saddle. The photograph showed the mare wearing the same blanket while being ridden by a small blonde girl of maybe six or seven.

She flipped over the photograph and, for the hundredth time, contemplated the printer's stamp, *Little Haven News—Print, Post, Daguerreotypes*, and the carefully written words, *Yellow Feather & Spirit, 1852*.

The photograph had been taken this year. Surely that was a sign as much as Spirit's unique markings. Here lay Faith's future. She'd always gained strength from helping others. Today would be no different.

She would ride Spirit to Little Haven and return the mare to the girl named Yellow Feather. A girl who—judging by how lovingly she smiled at Spirit —must surely be missing her.

But when Faith assessed the two paths ahead, her unease returned. Before finding Spirit, she'd seldom ridden. A boat and wagon had delivered her from the teacher's academy to Timber Creek. She eyed the puny sack slung over Spirit's shoulders. She'd stuffed it with her meager belongings and enough food for a week if rationed. She was ill-prepared for the journey ahead, not to mention the decisions she must make alone.

Spirit tossed her head and nickered, making Faith smile.

"You're right. I'm not alone. We're in this together. Until I must give you up." The thought made her body heavy with loss. She tucked her loneliness deep into a corner of her heart and the daguerreotype back into its pocket for safekeeping. "I'll keep you safe until we part ways," she promised as she resumed petting Spirit's neck. "I'm certain you'll do the same. You'll protect me like no one else can."

Spirit was no ordinary horse. When Faith found her and washed the mud and trail dust from her coat, she discovered Spirit's unusual coloring. Pure white except for a few patches of chestnut on her belly, it was the crown of brown covering her ears that marked her as a sacred Medicine Hat or spirit horse.

Native legend said that the rider of a Medicine Hat horse was protected. They couldn't be harmed by bullets or arrows, not even by lightning. Too bad Spirit's protection didn't include barbed words. Mrs. Cain and Mrs. Crisp's accusations still stung.

Indignation stiffened her spine. She wasn't immoral or ignorant. She'd recognized Spirit's worth not only from the daguerreotype but also from her mother's stories.

Her mother had Indian blood. Mrs. Cain and Mrs. Crisp didn't know that. No one did. It was Faith's secret...although her inky-black hair and high cheekbones probably made some speculate about her heritage.

Whoever had written the names Yellow Feather and Spirit on the back of the daguerreotype most likely had Indian blood as well. She'd locate the photographer in Little Haven, ask them where the girl lived, and return Spirit. Then she'd scan every word of the newspaper and find a new position doing whatever honest work was available.

She'd prove Mrs. Cain and Mrs. Crisp wrong, and Mr. Doolan too. She had prospects beyond the depraved and the desperate.

But first, she must complete this journey.

Her gaze darted between the two paths. Spirit edged toward the narrow trail that ascended to Bird's Eye Pass, making her choice clear.

Faith wasn't convinced. Wouldn't it be more prudent to take the flatter, more used, and therefore safer road?

Spirit's entire body tensed. She released a shrill whinny and trotted up the trail before Faith could pull her to a halt. High above them, a man on a pale horse galloped out of the mist cloaking the pass. Long dark hair flying out behind him, the man rode with an elegant grace as if one with his horse. His pace quickened, heading straight for her.

She urged Spirit back onto the main road. Her decision had been made for her. She didn't want to approach the rider thundering toward her with such determination.

Mustering her own resolve, she tried to make Spirit go faster. The best she achieved was a brisk walk. At least they moved away from the trail. With any luck, the rider would be heading toward Timber Creek.

His mount's galloping hoofbeats grew louder, pounded onto the main road, and then slowed to a clip-clop—trotting her way. Several agonizing heartbeats later, the horse's strides fell into an easy rhythm with Spirit's.

Surprise loosened Faith's lips. Without looking back, she asked, "Are you following me?"

"Yes." The timbre of his deep voice was pleasing but unusual. The orphanage and academy had accommodated many with mixed accents, but none as intriguing as his. A fanciful notion, since he'd said only one word. And not a word she should appreciate.

She strove to make her voice stern and unapproachable. "*Why* are you following me?"

"You are riding—" He heaved a sigh, then continued in a gentler tone like he feared he might spook her. "My horse."

Astonishment made her flinch. Her slight tug on the reins brought Spirit to a halt. Before she could stop the mare, she'd turned to touch noses with the man's horse.

Faith's gaze jumped from the horses' heads to

lock on him. His long hair no longer billowed out behind him, but fell poker-straight before disappearing behind his broad shoulders. Hair as black as hers. He shared her cheekbones as well, but higher. And while her skin was pale as snow, his was brown as a smooth pine cone—with not even a whisker, let alone the bushy beard and eyebrows Mr. Hammond and his fellow loggers possessed.

The man's sleek handsomeness mesmerized her until she saw the cruel scar marring his perfection. White and puckered with age, it cut from his left eye to the corner of his jaw. She gasped with regret for the pain he surely must have endured during its infliction.

Then she pressed her lips tight, embarrassed by her rudeness and audacity. She'd been staring at the man rather than responding to his words.

"I'm sorry. You are mistaken. This isn't your horse," she said in a rush. "She belongs to a little girl."

"The girl is..." His jaw tightened, making his scar stand out even more against his sun-burnished skin. "She is part of my family."

"No, she isn't. She's blonde and you're dark." Mortified at her bluntness, Faith clapped her palm over her mouth. She dropped her hand just as fast so she could explain. "I meant to say she cannot be your family anymore than she could be mine. You and I share the same black hair."

He nodded solemnly. "Native blood runs in your veins." He surveyed the road. "Your tribe is near?"

"I'm not—" She drew in a deep breath, then admitted what she'd never told anyone. "I cannot remember my tribe. I lost my mother at a young age. After that, I lived in several orphanages, a school for teachers, and until this morning, Timber Creek's logging camp."

He nodded again. "And where are you going now?"

"I'm returning Spirit to her rightful owner in Little Haven."

"Yellow Feather is not in Little Haven."

"You know her name." Awe rendered her voice as hushed as the mist ghosting the trees. Could he really be the little girl's relative?

His gaze was direct, but also dark with mystery. "I wish to know you as well." His reply held her spellbound, made her happy but also restless.

When she didn't answer, he reached inside his shirt and pulled out a daguerreotype of similar size to the one hidden in Spirit's riding blanket. In his picture, he crouched beside Yellow Feather while the little girl touched his scar.

Faith's eyes widened with amazement.

From under a furrowed brow, he contemplated the picture as well. "She would not agree to have her likeness captured unless I stayed by her side." He returned the picture to its pocket and its home close to his heart.

Yellow Feather loved this man. The feeling appeared to be mutual. The realization doubled his allure and the nervous energy building inside her. She held out her hand and hoped it was steady. "I'm Faith Featherby."

When his frown deepened and he didn't move to accept her greeting, she let her hand fall again. Her heart sank with it, dismayed at the thought of offending him with her ignorance of his ways. Maybe it wasn't customary for women in his tribe to be so bold. She certainly felt bold. She'd never been this talkative with anyone.

"Feather-B?" he asked, still frowning.

She couldn't seem to say or do anything that he liked. The familiar compulsion to retreat into silence rose inside her. She forced herself to say the first thing that came to mind. "Is there something wrong with my name?"

A smile tugged his lips, then disappeared so fast she wondered if she'd imagined it.

"It is a beautiful name." He bowed his head and laid his palm over the place where his and Yellow Feather's daguerreotype lay hidden. "I could not have picked a better one for you."

His reply gave her more pleasure than was appropriate. He was a stranger who'd yet to offer his name. "And you are?"

He opened his mouth, paused, and then said with quiet deliberation. "Eagle."

"Will you tell me where Yellow Feather is?"

"She is with my sister. I will take you to them."

The burst of euphoria inside her made everything around her seem brighter. "You will?"

"Yes. We should travel over the pass." His gaze rose to the mountain he'd ridden down. "The journey will be faster and safer."

Safer? She doubted that. Her teeth worried her bottom lip until she couldn't contain her uncertainty or her words. "Can we reach your sister and Yellow Feather via this road?"

"We can."

"Then I wish to continue in the direction I was going." She braced herself for an argument that would shatter whatever goodwill had grown between them.

"The choice is yours." He motioned for her to ride on. "Lead the way."

He'd agreed? She'd won. So why did she feel like she'd lost? "You won't ride beside me?"

"Better if I follow. If we meet anyone, you do not want to be seen riding beside me."

"Are you wanted by the law?" she asked, then

cringed and silently berated herself for asking something so foolish. If a man were an outlaw, he
wouldn't admit it.

"They hunt for me in the east, not here."

His reply left her blinking with shock. She
should be afraid of him, but she wasn't. Had his trou-
bles with the authorities resulted in his scar? "If
you're not hiding from anyone, why not ride
beside me?"

"Because you are white, and I am not."

"But the blood of both people beats in my heart.
You recognized that right away."

"Your beauty will blind most from seeing that
truth." His compliment brought heat to her cheeks,
but his next words iced her veins. "Spirit may be a
Medicine Horse, but you are still not safe riding
beside me. No one is."

CHAPTER 3

*R*iding ahead of Eagle, Faith strained to hear the thump of his horse's hooves, craving reassurance that he wasn't a figment of her imagination. That he still followed her.

A miracle in the form of a very attractive man had ridden out of the mist to join her journey. The man had allowed her to continue riding Spirit even though he claimed the horse was his. He'd let her decide which path to take. He'd called her beautiful.

He was too good to be real.

Maybe he wasn't. Her mother's stories had included ghost tales as well. In them, each person had a good and bad *tamahnous* following them. At first glance, Eagle had appeared too fierce to approach, but he'd shown her only kindness. Whether apparition or man, she could do the same.

The darkness in his eyes made her believe he needed a link to the living.

A barrage of shouts echoed in the trees ahead. Voices raised in disagreement. The curve in the road concealed whoever approached, but the wall of ever-greens wouldn't protect her much longer. The voices grew louder, joined by the rattle of bridles, the creak of saddle leather and the clatter of shod hooves, drowning out the quieter ones behind her.

She peered over her shoulder and found—nothing. Her *tamahnous* spirit man had vanished.

An eerie silence descended. Not even a bird chirped in the trees circling her like a cage. A cold dread raised goose bumps on her skin as she spun to face what lay ahead.

Only two horse lengths separated her from a pair of scraggly-bearded, dirt-stained, and ragged-clothed men sitting on equally unkempt horses. They gaped at her for a long moment. Then their eyes narrowed, and they grinned, baring blackened teeth.

The thinner man's snakelike eyes never left her as he leaned sideways on his saddle and spat a stream of tobacco on the earth. "*Tu t'plains encore qu'c'est la mauvaise route?*"

What had he said? Something about complaining?

Even though a friend at the teacher's academy

had taught her enough French to hold a conversation, her panicked brain balked at entering this one. Oblivion was tempting, but foolish. She concentrated on listening carefully so she could translate whatever they said next.

Snake Eyes' partner scratched his chin with a three-fingered hand. "*Mon erreur. T'as choisi la bonne route, mon ami.*"

My mistake. You chose the right road, my friend.

Faith disagreed. She wished with all her heart they'd chosen a different one. She certainly should have. Taxing terrain, wild beasts, and the complete unknown was safer than a road that now threatened to suffocate her with terror and worse.

She forced a smile, hoping it would conceal her fear and the falsehood that sprang to mind for extracting herself from the men's company. She added an eager tone to her French as she said, "The right road for all of us. For miles my traveling companions have talked of meeting someone to break our journey's monotony. I only rode ahead to rest my ears."

Snake Eyes scanned the road behind her.

She gestured for them to go around her and said in French, "They'll want to meet you."

Three Fingers huffed out a dubious laugh. "*Y z'ont pas c'qu'on veut.*"

They don't have what we want.

Everyone wanted something. The pile of furs strapped to the men's saddles caught her interest. Driven by her hope that she could convince them to leave, her French tumbled out fast. "You'll wish to trade with my friends. They carry our supplies. As you can see"—she pointed to the sack in front of her —"I carry very little. I have nothing of value."

Three Fingers glanced at his friend. "*T'en penses quoi?*"

What do you think?

She hoped they'd think about leaving.

"*J'pense...*" Snake Eyes tightened his grip on his reins. "*...qu'on la tire dans les bois et on évalue c'qui s'cache sous sa robe.*"

Her mind balked again. She didn't want to accept what he'd said. But the words were as clear as they were horrifying.

We drag her into the woods and we evaluate what's under her dress.

Snake Eyes urged his horse toward her. Three Fingers did the same.

Fear paralyzed Faith, but not Spirit. Flattening her dark ears against her head, the mare bit the closest man's horse, then kicked the other with her front hoof. The usually calm mare's wild movements nearly unseated Faith. Dropping her reins, she grabbed Spirit's mane and whatever else she could clutch—which happened to be the sack.

While Three Fingers waved his hands in Spirit's face, Snake Eyes dodged her fury and reached for Faith. She raised the sack like a shield against his grasping hands. He yanked it from her hold and snared her wrist in a grip so bruising that she cried out.

The wind whistled in her ears. So did a high-pitched shriek.

Her captor released her and grabbed his leg instead. The shaft of an arrow protruded from a hole in his thigh, leaking bright red blood.

The trees came alive with shouts, whooping like a hundred heathens closing in. More arrows whipped by, striking legs, arms, and shoulders. Miraculously, none hit her or the horses. Snake Eyes tried to hide behind her sack. Its paltry size didn't help him.

A yelp or grunt followed each arrow strike. Until the two men spun their mounts around and fled without a backward glance.

The moment they did, Eagle and his pale horse bounded from the trees. Guiding his mount with only his legs, they skidded to a halt in front of her. He held a bow with an arrow notched and strung tight, aimed in the direction the men had departed.

"I thought I'd dreamed you." Relief that she hadn't made her slump against Spirit's now calm and steady body.

Eagle's gaze remained on the empty road. "What was in the sack they took?"

His question confounded her. Then she remembered—the sack she'd attempted to use as a shield and lost in the process. "It held all of my belongings." The dire nature of that loss made her throat clench. "They took my food."

"You will not go hungry. I will give you what I have."

She contemplated the single pack tied to the back of the blanket that formed Eagle's saddle, a blanket similar to Spirit's. "You brought enough for two?"

When he shook his head, his long hair rippled like an inky waterfall. "No."

"I didn't think so."

"And..." When he said no more, she urged Spirit forward to stand beside him. The frown twisting his brow as he glared at the bend around which her attackers had disappeared stole her breath—but not her desire to learn what he'd been about to say.

"And what?" she prompted.

"I brought only enough for the briefest of journeys. I intended to cross the pass to Timber Creek and head straight back. A two-day trip."

"How much longer is the main road?"

Eagle studied her from the corner of his eye but remained silent.

"Twice as long?"

He shrugged one shoulder and stared at the road ahead again. He still held an arrow notched in his bow, on guard for the men who'd left but might return...as soon as they pulled the arrows from their bodies and found their courage or, more likely, their desire for revenge. If they found her or Eagle, they'd both suffer the consequences. They needed to finish their journey as swiftly as possible.

"Tell me the truth. Please...speak to me."

"This road will require three times the number of days," he replied. "But you will not go hungry no matter how long the journey. That I vow."

She tried to sit as straight and confident on Spirit as Eagle looked sitting beside her on his horse. "I've changed my mind about going forward on this road."

His sigh overflowed with resignation. "I understand. You wish to return to Timber Creek."

"No. I wish to take the faster route. Then neither of us need go without." Or would have to defend themselves against people who didn't believe in human decency or legends written in the crown of brown covering Spirit's ears.

Still, she had as many preconceptions to overcome as the trappers, woodsmen, and school committees of this land. She needed to do what she advised her students. She needed to open her mind.

"It's time I faced the unknown."

CHAPTER 4

*A*head of Eagle, on a single-file trail that soared steeply before gentling to hug the mountainside, rode a woman whose soft-spoken manner captivated him as much as her determination. He'd happily follow her anywhere and for any number of days. One day on this mist-shrouded path would end too soon.

Was that why he'd so easily agreed to use the longer road?

He'd been selfish. He'd put her life in peril. Here in the Far West's thick forests, danger could lurk anywhere—waiting to leap out and hurt Faith Featherby. So could the dark spirit hounding him. He'd left his people on the faraway plains to spare them the wrath of the soldiers who'd named him their quarry. He'd never escape the turmoil that followed him and eventually hurt everyone close to him.

Turmoil he made worse with his temper.

But as soon as he'd found Faith, she'd calmed him like no one else had. Until he'd been forced to fight evil with evil again.

He knew only a handful of French words. *Bonjour* and *ami* were two of them. Those men hadn't said hello, and they were friends to nobody but themselves. Other than speaking French rather than English, Faith's attackers had been no different from the trappers who'd murdered his mother and Osage sister.

He'd been an arrow away from ending their lives as well and revealing the biggest threat sitting an arm's length away from Faith. The savage inside him. But his rage had been restrained. His arrows had hit their marks. He hadn't drawn his rifle. And the malice that had risen in his heart had left with the men.

Maybe he'd changed. Or maybe he'd merely gotten better at concealing his true nature, even from himself.

Whatever the case, Faith Featherby deserved more than he could ever provide. The profound loneliness in her voice told him so. She'd find no happiness wandering the woods with only him following her.

She needed a place she could call home.

He'd leave her as soon as he delivered her to his only close family who still walked this earth. Blue Sky held the means to sheltering both the child and the woman he'd stumbled upon while trying to avoid people. One more day, then he'd vanish forever in the forest.

"Why did you...disappear into the trees?" Faith's question, so similar to his thoughts, startled him. As did her tone. It held no accusation, only the desire to understand.

"Your departure frightened me as much as the men's arrival," she added.

"Fear is a powerful force. So is surprise."

"They can be friend and foe." A bend in the trail allowed him a glimpse of the smile curving her lips as she said, "A shield and a sword."

Her happiness combined with her ability to understand him, when so many could not, filled him with hope. "Yes. If we look with clear eyes, the Great Spirit's gifts appear all around us, including tools to protect..." He searched for the words to describe Faith Featherby. She was one of the Great Spirit's most beautiful creations. He wished he had an infinite number of days to not only explain his feelings but show her as well.

Under the creak of the treetops swaying high above in the breeze, her soft-spoken words once more bridged the silence between them. "You left for the same reason you wouldn't ride beside me. You say it's not safe." Her voice became uncharacteristically sharp. "I see things differently. Spirit does as well. She was happy to see you. She trusts you."

He strove for both an honest and an impartial reply. "Spirit trusts you more. Other than Yellow Feather, I have never watched her carry anyone so carefully or, when you were attacked, defend them so fiercely. She is not an easy horse to ride."

If Spirit decided she didn't like her rider, she'd brush them off by passing too close to a tree or simply buck until they parted ways. Spirit cared for this woman as much as for the six-year-old girl who refused to speak and tell Eagle why she'd been alone in the woods when he'd found her.

Spirit had a soft spot for orphans with good hearts. He only fit half that description. Faith was as compassionate as she was beautiful. In a world where he'd endured almost every injury known to man, she worried that her words might wound him.

"Why did you...use only your arrows and not your rifle to...battle those men?"

Her halting, carefully worded questions made him realize she was nervous asking them. She'd told him she wished to face the *unknown*. He might not be able to give her all she deserved, but he could help her in this particular quest.

"A rifle is a weapon of last resort. It can be heard for miles. If trouble slumbers nearby, it will be drawn to the sound and you."

The snapping of branches on the steep slope above them made him prime his bow with an arrow aimed in that direction.

Both horses halted and pricked their ears toward the continued commotion, which now included snorting. A rack of antlers as tall as Eagle's bow rose above a thicket of dogwood. A wide-eyed elk—with evidence of its interrupted grazing dangling from its mouth—shook its antlers in warning. Their deadly sharp points far outnumbered his arrows.

"She looks irate as a momma bear," Faith whispered. "Have we come between her and her young?"

"Not *her*, but *him*," he replied just as quietly. "The autumn rut turns bull elks belligerent when courting females. His mate is hidden nearby."

"He's protecting her." Admiration filled Faith's voice, but to her credit, she spoke no louder than before. "Have we separated them?"

"If we had, he'd already have charged." Eagle kept his bow drawn and ready as the elk stomped a stride closer down the mountainside. "Remain still. He needs to believe we pose no threat."

"If we cannot move, what can we do?"

On the narrow trail, their options were limited. They could wait for the elk to retreat, an unlikely outcome since they'd invaded his territory. Or they could ride slowly onward and hope he allowed them to leave without deciding to show off his prowess.

If he did, a well-aimed arrow or bullet might stop his obstinate heart, but not before he slashed Faith with his sharp antlers or crushed her beneath his massive weight. Eagle needed to put a barricade between her and the elk. If the trail weren't so narrow and the terrain so steep, he'd already be using his body.

From the corner of his eye, he searched the path ahead. "Everything we do must be slow and deliberate. Turn little by little until you face forward again."

When she did as requested, he said, "Do you see the twin cedars to the right of the path?"

"Yes."

"As soon as they are between you and the elk, ask Spirit to stop."

Using his knees, he eased his own mount forward, encouraging Spirit to do the same. Their movement caused the elk to move as well, more angry head swaying and stomps down the slope. Until they halted, and so did the elk.

"These trees aren't big enough." Faith's gaze jumped from the trunks to him. "We must continue until we find cover for both of us."

He disagreed. As long as she was safe, he wasn't moving. "We wait till he calms."

"I see another pair of stalwart trees ahead."

"It's too far."

"I can make it and make space for you here."

"You'll get hurt."

"Spirit will keep me safe."

Their flurry of increasingly hurried words made the elk pin back his ears and shred a nearby sapling with his antlers.

"If you're knocked from Spirit's back," Eagle said in a tranquil tone at odds with the alarm surging in his veins, "she cannot protect you." The thought that he might fail Faith as well made his hands shake. He tightened his grip on his bow. "We stay as we are."

"I won't sit and watch while you're attacked."

The elk turned his antlers on an aspen's sturdy trunk and, snorting with each swipe, sent its bark flying.

"No more talking until he calms down."

"I know nothing about elks," Faith said in a voice as hushed as it was determined, "but this Romeo sounds far from calming. So...if you won't come with me, I'll go on alone." Her chin rose stubbornly. So did her heels, preparing to tell Spirit to abandon her sanctuary.

"Wait—"

A mighty bellow silenced him. The elk lunged toward him. Full speed. Head down. Antlers hiding most of his chest. But not his heart.

A difficult shot. His only choice. He released his arrow.

At the same time, Spirit's hooves thundered along the trail. The elk skidded to a halt with his nose brushing the ground. Eagle's arrow pinged off his bone-hard antlers, which then swung Faith's way. The elk rocked back on his haunches, preparing to charge her.

Eagle hollered and waved his bow in a wide arc. The elk's attention snapped back to him. As soon as it did, Eagle urged his mount behind the cedars Faith had abandoned.

Ahead of him, Faith sat safely on Spirit behind her new barricade. Her relieved smile soothed his racing heart, but the distance now separating them did not. What if the elk moved between them?

The crackling of underbrush told him the elk was on the move again. And moving fast.

With a whooping shout, Eagle sent his mount sprinting forward. A blur barreled down the incline, threatening to broadside him. He lashed out with his bow. Another bellow rang in his ears, this one full of fury and pain.

Eagle yanked his horse to a halt behind Spirit, between Faith and the elk. Now free of the under-brush, the elk straddled the trail with his head hung low. Blood dripped from his tender-skinned nose onto the dirt. The cut would leave a scar. Better that than a hole in his ornery heart.

Choose another course. Turn away, Eagle silently urged the creature. *And I shall do the same.*

Other than his puffing nostrils and heaving sides, the elk didn't move. A slender-boned female peaked around him. Her guardian lifted his head and pawed the trail, churning up the bloodstained earth.

Eagle reached for another arrow. Pain lanced his arm and stopped him short of his goal. He tried again. His continued failure left him empty-handed with his breath hissing between his teeth.

"What's wrong?" Faith's words brushed the back of his neck, soft as a feather in flight. Gone too quick. But her grip on his shoulder was firm.

His gaze locked on her small hand, heating his flesh even with his shirt between them. He didn't care to look anywhere else.

She shook him. "Eagle, answer me. Are you hurt?"

Something warm dripped onto his thigh. Blood ran down his shirtsleeve from a gash in the cloth and his arm. "When I thrust my bow in the elk's face, we cut each other."

The wound would require attention, and soon.

If the elk chose to take his mate and leave now,

Eagle would live and bear a new scar. That outcome held little interest. He had one concern. His injury would prevent him from protecting the woman holding him so steadfastly.

She'd said she was prepared to go on alone, to leave him. But now she didn't budge.

Neither did the elk.

Yanking his rifle free of its case, he struggled to both cock and steady the weapon with one hand. Another hand joined him. Faith's slender fingers drew back the hammer, then settled around his. Her skin flush against his. No more barriers. Not cloth or indecision. He'd been a fool not to take her hand earlier when she'd offered it in greeting.

With her support, the rifle became solid as the mountain beneath them. Faith gave him her strength and conviction. She gave him more than he'd ever dreamed possible. She gave him her grace.

Together they aimed in unspoken agreement. Their shot boomed above the elks' heads, then echoed in the trees amid a flurry of raucous squawking. The female elk bounded down the slope, once again vanishing into the forest. After a brief hesitation, her mate followed.

Only the magpies' startled voices lingered. A beacon for trouble. Like the retort of his rifle.

The realization made him stiffen. As soon as he did, Faith released his hand. She reined Spirit around him to stare at his wound. The worry in her wide eyes, along with her paler than usual face, spurred him into action.

He needed to prepare for the next battle to protect her.

CHAPTER 5

*E*agle returned his rifle to its case and dug one-handed in the pack behind him.

"What are you searching for?" Faith asked.

"Needle and thread."

"You plan to stitch yourself up with one hand?"

He had no other choice—until she grasped his hand again. Her gentle touch rendered him unable to resist as she lifted his hand. When she saw the spider tattoo on his palm, she inhaled sharply with curiosity and more questions.

She didn't speak until she placed his palm above his wound, and then only to give an instruction. "Press here to slow the bleeding while I do the searching." She cleared her throat roughly. "And the stitching." After she'd found and threaded the needle, she enlarged the hole in his shirtsleeve to better see his wound. When she did, she swallowed hard, and her gaze darted up to meet his.

"You can do anything you set your mind to," he reassured her. "But this..." This was asking too much of her. "I can wait until we reach—"

"You cannot wait, and neither can I. My mind is fixed on helping you. It also shies away from the thought of causing you more pain."

The determination and uncertainty furrowing her brow pinched his heart. "Concentrate on how each stitch slows my bleeding. Your hands give me life." The desire to keep her in his life made him lean closer to her.

Faith wisely stayed where she was. "You'll tell me if I should stop?"

He nodded. Not in agreement, but in acceptance.

The first stitch burned like fire. He gritted his teeth and focused on Faith's face, committing her bravery and beauty to memory, giving her a permanent home in his heart. Her hands never wavered until she finished and sat back to stare at his blood on them.

He handed her his water canteen.

While she washed her hands, she said, "We should wrap your wound. Do you have bandages in your pack?"

"No." Her frown made him hasten to add, "We shall find what we need at my sister's home."

"All that I need is here." Her words astonished him. And her, too. Her cheeks glowed an enticing pink. She kept her gaze lowered as she returned his canteen. "What I meant to say is I can use my petticoat."

The word was unfamiliar. He swiftly learned its meaning when Faith raised the hem of her heavy wool skirt to reveal a garment as fluffy and white as a summer cloud. When his gaze shot up to study her face, her blush had gone scarlet. The women from his world wore fewer layers than those raised in white settlements, but they were no less modest.

Wishing to ease her discomfort, he stared at his arm.

The row of neat stitches was impressive. The scar would be faint. He'd treasure it forever. During the long, lonely years ahead, he'd cherish every reminder of the woman who'd somehow become the center of his world in less than a day.

"Ready?" Faith held up his bandages. Her embarrassment hadn't stopped her from tearing an ample swath from her underclothing. Cloth that would carry her warmth.

He held out his arm, eager to feel her touch and form another memory to hold close.

Her fingertips skimmed his skin, soft as a newly born leaf. He craved more. He tried not to lean toward her again. Looming over her like a lusty elk wouldn't help either of them.

"I'm sorry," she said.

Her apology baffled him. "You have nothing to be sorry for."

"I'm causing you more pain."

She'd misinterpreted the return of his rigid posture.

"The good news is," she added before he could form a reply, "I'm done."

He examined his bandaged arm. The binding had been accomplished as tidily as the stitching. "You have mended people before."

She shrugged and fidgeted with her skirt, making sure it once more covered her petticoat. "Only minor cuts on tiny limbs."

"You have a mother's heart."

"I wish. I've only tended other people's children."

The melancholy in her voice puzzled him. He was certain of only one thing. "They were fortunate to have you."

She didn't reply. She stared at neither the path ahead nor behind, but the ground beneath them.

Her sudden silence fed his confusion and concern. "After you return Spirit, will you retrace your steps to Timber Creek?"

Her gaze remained downcast. "I'm heading to Little Haven to start a new life."

Too many men there would be keen to be part of her life, in any way they could. Men like the trappers. A primal surge of protectiveness obliterated rational thought. He wanted to butt heads with any man who dared come near her.

He and the elk had officially become spirit brothers.

Faith wasn't safe near him or in Little Haven. She should stay with his sister. Then he could watch over her from a distance until she found the right man. But what if that man had already found Faith? What if he waited for her in Little Haven?

The idea unsettled him as well. But it was only a stray thought. She hadn't said anything about— His gut clenched. She'd mentioned a name.

"Are you traveling to Little Haven to meet Romeo?"

Wide with bewilderment, her gaze finally met his. "Why do you say that?"

"You mentioned the name when speaking about the elk."

Laughter spilled from her lips like a spring from the earth, unexpected but very welcome. "I'd forgotten. The elk's stubborn passion reminded me of Romeo. He's a character in a tale of fate and chance and, above all, love."

Eagle's list of spirit brothers was growing.

"Most of my knowledge comes from stories I've

read or heard my mother recite." The determination in Faith's sigh caressed his ears. "From now on I'm resolved to look for wisdom in everything around me."

Her gaze went to his palm and its tattoo. "What does it mean?"

"A spider is a symbol of strength among the Osage. My family tattooed its web over our hearts because that is where spiders and family make their home...even when they drift away in life and death."

Eyes wide and lips slightly parted, Faith leaned toward him as if she hung on his every word.

"Blue Sky was the first to request the spider on her palm. She said if she put her hand to her heart, the spider would find its web and she'd bring her loved ones close again. My mother and Osage sister are here." He pressed his palm to his heart.

Faith bowed her head and mimicked his movement. "Home is where the heart is."

He'd been a grown man when his family had been killed. Faith had mentioned losing her mother at a young age...just like Yellow Feather. The pair could help each other in ways he never could. With the gift of Faith's quiet tenacity, Yellow Feather would grow into a strong woman. His heart ached to see that transformation, to be part of that journey.

He was being selfish again. The only journey he'd ever share with Faith was today.

"Thank you," he said, "for mending my injury."

"Try to avoid straining your arm for a while. No more using your bow or rifle. I see why you called it a weapon of last resort. It was extremely loud." Alarm widened her eyes. She scanned the trees surrounding them. "What if someone heard? What if more trouble comes looking for us? I don't think I could shoot a person."

"Taking a life hardens the soul. That will not be your future. I promise."

She went very still. "You've taken lives?"

"Yes." Luckily, he'd regained his senses before he'd ended the life of a loved one.

For the second time, Faith studied the scar on his face. She'd guessed he hadn't received that mark by accident. The rest was a mystery her limited experience couldn't solve. She deserved the unabridged story. No matter how ugly.

"I killed the men who gave me this." He rubbed the scar as it prickled with the phantom pain of its birth.

"Did they...attack you first?" She was back to being nervous about her questions.

He shared her apprehension. Once he told her, she'd be keen to leave him as quickly as possible. "I let them. I also gave them no choice but to attack."

She shook her head. "There's always a choice."

"Not after they killed my mother and Osage

sister. From that moment, their lives hung by a thread."

Faith's eyes had gone wide as an owl's.

"I cut them loose. I still carry that knife." He tapped the leg of his left moccasin and the sheathed blade hidden there.

"Another weapon of last resort." Her calm reply made his head spin. "To defeat two foes with only a knife, you'd have to get close."

"I became their shadow. If they had numbered more than two, I would have departed this world with them."

She shivered and searched the trees until her gaze halted on the faint glow of the sun descending toward a horizon still hidden behind the mist. He had to hurry Faith toward her destination. She needed the warm hearth and safe haven of his sister's home.

"We should ride on." Ignoring his own advice, he stayed put. He wanted only to take Faith in his arms and shelter her with his embrace. "When darkness falls on this path, it will not be safe for either of us." *Especially with me wanting to hold you and never let you go.*

CHAPTER 6

*D*espite Eagle's violent past and fears for a similar future, his decision to finally ride beside Faith when the trail widened was the greatest of gifts. Being close to him filled her with a limitless vitality...which unfortunately led to an even greater trepidation.

Eagle wasn't a ghost. He was a man made of flesh and blood. His blood had flowed through her fingers. She didn't want to contemplate a tomorrow without him on Earth.

He'd fought enough battles with foes willing to drag him into the spirit world. He'd earned the right to find peace in this life. He needed a sanctuary, and she was determined to help him build one strong enough to shelter both him and Yellow Feather.

Reaching his sister's home was the first and most important step.

"How long before we arrive at your sister's?"

"Not more than a half-hour."

A long silence, with only the wind rustling the leaves, stretched between them. She strove to keep it that way. She examined the forest, hunting for any sign of a threat. The allure of the man riding beside her made her task difficult. When she snuck a peek at him, she found his gaze on her.

"You have no more questions?" he asked.

She shook her head. "I'm brimming with questions, but I must wait until we reach your sister's home."

"Why?"

"You said trouble was drawn to noise. You were right."

"Your voice is not *noise*." He sounded affronted by her comparison. "It is like...the breeze in the trees or the music of a bird."

His favorable opinion made her heart race with pleasure until she remembered her mission to put his safety first. She pressed her lips tight.

"You are the song that makes life better," he said in a huskily vehement tone.

Surprise broke her resolve not to speak. She shifted her seat on Spirit to better face him. "You cannot believe that. If I'd kept quiet and hadn't asked so many questions, maybe the elk wouldn't have become so upset. You wouldn't have got hurt. We wouldn't have had to fire your rifle."

"Or if we had been silent, we might have startled the elk more than we did. He would have charged immediately and given us no time to gather the tools to dissuade him."

"Tools like—" She bit her lip in indecision.

"A shield in the shape of trees and a rifle fired as a last resort. We did what we had to."

"You didn't have to shoot over the elk's head." That he'd spared the animal's life pleased her. His actions were as kind as his words.

His voice remained as somber as his attention riveted on the trail. "I have seen too many die needlessly." He halted his horse, and Spirit stopped as well. A small smile curved his mouth as he thrust his chin toward the trail ahead. "Now here is a subject worthy of a question."

A fallen tree blocked their path.

When she remained silent, he said, "My first question is... What are you thinking?"

His teasing tone made her grin. "That's an awfully wide trunk for a horse to step over."

He nodded. "Our horses will need to jump."

The memory of Spirit lunging at the trappers obliterated her good humor. "The last time Spirit did anything more lively than a trot, I nearly fell off."

"If you wish to dismount and climb over, Spirit will follow. You can remount on the other side."

Vines and brambles covered the ends of the trunk. The tree had lain there for a while. "I could do that, but"—her smile returned—"I have a question first. What did you do when you reached this part of the trail on your way to Timber Creek?"

"I kept my seat and asked my horse to jump over."

"How did you do that?" She was especially interested in the *keeping her seat* part.

"Loosen your reins and lean forward."

With a will of its own, her body followed his instructions.

"Hold tight to Spirit's mane and even tighter to her belly with your legs."

As soon as she did, Spirit eased into a trot that accelerated into a leap. Buoyant as a cloud, they soared over the trunk. Effortless. Exhilarating. But not endless. On the other side, the trail rose up to meet them.

Spirit's hooves struck the ground. The impact jolted Faith forward, then back. She bounced hard enough to rattle her teeth. Her legs lost their grip. She slid sideways. Only her grasp on Spirit's mane slowed her descent.

Eagle and his horse were beside her again. He held out his uninjured arm, ready to catch her.

She yanked herself back up onto her seat. A surge of relief, followed quickly by pride, rose inside her. She drew Spirit to a halt so she could share her elation with Eagle. "I feel like I could jump anything now. Thank you for showing me how."

Eagle's previously muted smiles coalesced into an unrestrained grin that dazzled her with his joy. "Spirit could not have chosen a better rider."

"I bounced too much, though, and nearly fell. How do I stop that from happening again?"

"Practice every day."

"I will." Her shoulders slumped. Tomorrow she wouldn't be able to share the outcome with him. She also wouldn't have a horse to ride.

"What's wrong?" He nudged his mount closer until their knees nearly touched.

His radiant smile had vanished, but the warmth of his body and spirit remained. Not for long. Her heart would mourn, but never regret. "I will always be glad you rode with me today."

"No finer place exists than the path by your side." His words lifted her morale until she felt like she was airborne again.

"When Spirit arrived winded and lame in Timber Creek, I told everyone that she deserved a second chance, that everyone deserves one. I didn't realize it at the time, but Spirit was giving me a chance. The chance to meet you. I'll always remember you. You have a home in my heart."

"So do you." The warmth of his hand comforted hers as he raised it to his chest and held it there. Her hand lay between his spider-tattooed palm and the web hidden under his shirt. Beneath the soft buckskin and the solid wall of his chest his heart thumped strong and fast.

"Your heart is racing," she whispered.

"Today it beats only for you." He dropped her hand and jerked back. "I should not have said that."

She caught his face between her palms and halted his retreat. Neither his scar nor the rigid planes of his face daunted her.

"My heartache is a future I will not share with you." He closed his eyes, depriving her of their dark mystery.

"It's too late to hide. You've shown me too much. On the outside, you are like the mountain, tough and impenetrable. Inside you are a tree in the wind, swaying with compassion and wisdom. The closer we get, the steadier I become. You make me stronger."

A frown tormented his brow. "Strength can be an illusion. Didn't your mother's stories include the raven?"

"He's the trickster."

"Yes. A raven delights in gliding down to hop

around us on the ground, giving the illusion it is the safest of places. But when danger approaches, he will not hesitate to soar skyward again and watch from a distance."

She tightened her hold on him. "Let him fly wherever he wants. He cannot take away the truth. Danger has arrived twice. Each time we stayed together. I'm the better for it and...I'm finally happy."

His eyes popped open. Hope flickered in their depths before the shadows returned. "You must look for someone who will *keep* you happy."

"After one day with you, it's illogical to believe I cannot find happiness without you. My heart understands what my head cannot. Today I'm alive. If we part, I will fade to a shadow of what could've been."

"You are young and resilient. You will go on."

"When you first appeared, I wondered if you were real. Now I see the truth. Until today, I was the ghost. I don't want to go on merely existing and getting by. I want a tomorrow overflowing with life and love." When she drew him closer, he didn't resist. "I want that future with you."

The forest crackled and crunched louder than when the elk had charged. Three young men on foot leapt out to circle them with their rifles. They shared Eagle's dark hair and bronzed complexion, but pockmarks instead of a knife wound scarred their faces.

And hate narrowed their eyes as they glared down their gun barrels at them.

Eagle slowly pushed her away until he slipped from her grasp.

A horrible realization stabbed her heart. The men's weapons were not aimed at her but solely at Eagle. And he was distancing himself from her to ensure they remained that way.

CHAPTER 7

The men may have pointed their guns at Eagle, but they darted sullen glances at Faith and Spirit. The mare did not move. She did not bite or kick, like she'd done with the trappers. Nor did she prick her ears with curiosity, like she'd done with the elk. She only trembled.

Faith laid a comforting hand on her neck. "Spirit knows them."

"I do as well," Eagle replied in a grim tone. "I saw two of them prowling around my sister's home. When they ran off, I went to check on Spirit. She was gone."

Their hushed conversation brought no comment from the men.

Outrage curled her hands into fists. "They tried to ride her, and she did everything she could to escape them. Until she went lame and they discarded her."

"Then they heard, as I did, that a horse with her coloring was in a logging camp, a location guarded by many men wielding axes. They had to wait for Spirit to leave before attempting to make her theirs again. She will never let them."

"Can you explain that to them?"

"I am Osage. They are Molalla."

The word Molalla made the men stiffen and start their own exchange of muttered words she couldn't decipher.

"We do not speak the same tongue," Eagle continued. "It would not matter if we did. They are blinded by their hunger for Spirit's sacred power and their anger that she shares it with others and not them. But they cannot harm you as long as you stay seated on her."

A cold apprehension crept up her spine. "What about you?"

Eagle shifted his uninjured arm until his palm rested on his left leg, a hand's-breadth away from the top of his knee-high moccasin and the hidden blade that had scarred him for life. "My future is here. Yours is on the downhill trail branch ahead. When you reach my sister and Yellow Feather, tell them—"

"You'll tell them yourself because there's always

been room for you with me"—she reached behind herself and patted Spirit's rump—"on Spirit."

The men's conversation halted abruptly. They couldn't make sense of her words, but they understood her gesture.

The men sprang toward them, and Faith seized Spirit's mane with both hands. Spirit darted close to Eagle's mount. When the men jabbed their rifles butt-first between the two horses, Spirit flinched and sprang the other way.

She left Faith behind. Grasping only the air, Faith plummeted earthward.

A strong arm caught her and pulled her up to sit on Spirit again. The same arm cradled her against a solid chest with a wildly thumping heart. On a horse with a battle-scarred warrior sitting behind her, she'd found her perfect home.

One of their adversaries raised his rifle again. He aimed not at them but at Spirit.

Eagle's hand leapt from her waist to his leg, and then whipped toward the man. A flash of silver flew from his fingertips to plunge deep into the man's shoulder. The man cried out and stumbled back. His rifle barrel swung down. Its blast gouged the earth and rumbled the air.

The injured man couldn't balance his heavy rifle any better than Eagle. He tossed it aside and seized the knife handle protruding from his flesh. With a sneer that grew into a snarl, he yanked the blade free and lunged at Spirit's heart.

A barrage of arrows and bullets pummeled him mid-leap. Spine arched in agony, he pitched forward face first. The force of his fall thrust Eagle's blade into the ground. The hand that had released it lay limp and lifeless.

The man's cohorts dropped their rifles and fell on their knees, heads bowed, hands raised. As soon as they did, a dozen warriors armed with an assortment of bows and rifles stepped from their hiding places in the trees.

"Who are they?" Faith whispered.

"They are also Molalla." His calm tone as well as his words mystified her.

"How do you know?"

"See the oldest man with the gray hair?"

The man in question continued walking toward them while the others halted. A scar not unlike Eagle's marred his face. A face as pockmarked as their three attackers and most of the other men who'd saved them.

"His name is Gray Owl," Eagle said. "I met him when I searched for Yellow Feather's parents."

The old man stopped beside them. Faith laid a comforting hand on Spirit's neck again, but the mare's fear was gone. She nickered and nudged the man with her nose until he stroked her face. His kind gaze studied first Eagle and then Faith.

"Hello," she said. "Thank you for helping us."

The old man smiled and replied in a heavily accented voice, "Hello."

"He speaks English?" Disbelief made her glance over her shoulder to seek confirmation from Eagle.

He shook his head. "Only a few words."

When her shoulders drooped, his hand found hers and squeezed reassuringly. "Words are not necessary to be his friend. Spirit was with him when we first met. I showed him Yellow Feather's picture. When he saw it, his jaw dropped. Then he smiled as he does now. He pointed to himself and said his name. After I told him mine, he handed me Spirit's reins and walked away."

"That's why you said she was your horse."

"Not for long. When I returned to my sister's home, Yellow Feather raced out to hug me and Spirit as well. I gladly gave her the reins. She spoke for the first and only time. She laid her hand on her chest and said, *Yellow Feather*."

The old man continued stroking Spirit, listening to words that brought not a hint of understanding to his expression.

"Do you think he knows something about her parents?" Faith asked.

"Yes. But I cannot understand what he has tried

to tell me. Our only familiar words were greetings." Eagle paused and addressed the old man. "Hello, Gray Owl."

"Hello. *Bonjour*," Gray Owl said with a sigh, as if remembering that failed conversation.

"*Bonjour? Vous parlez français?*" More words spilled from Faith's lips, eager and hopeful, and all in French. "Who taught you? Can you talk to me? I have so many questions."

Gray Owl's smile widened with her every word. "I will give you answers if I can. I learned French from my friends, the Rousseaus." His mouth flattened into a grim line. "But I can no longer speak with them. They are gone."

She translated his words into English so Eagle could follow their conversation, then added, "I'm suddenly unsure what I should ask next. What if I don't know enough French to pick the right words?"

Eagle squeezed her hand again. "I have watched you succeed in every challenge you have faced. This will be no different."

The old man watched them keenly but waited patiently for her to speak again. His men were equally silent.

She translated her thoughts into French. "These men..." She indicated the three who'd attacked them. "Why did they endanger the life of a sacred horse?"

A grimace twisted the old man's battered face. When he spoke, he paused often to let her translate so Eagle would understand. "My sorrow is deep that they threatened her and you as well. Her choice of rider can be difficult for some to accept. My people's anger grew with the coming of the smallpox." He touched the pockmarks on his face. "Many loved ones died. But a bitter heart only brings more death. I will not let this be our legacy."

The last word was unfamiliar.

When she asked what it meant, he gestured in a wide arc around him. "The world we give to the children who survive."

"Thank you for giving Spirit to Eagle, so he could give her to Yellow Feather."

He stared at her blankly. "Who is Yellow Feather?"

Her own confusion made her turn to Eagle again for assistance. "He doesn't recognize Yellow Feather's name."

Eagle pulled his daguerreotype from his shirt pocket.

"A new name for a new family," Gray Owl said with a sad smile. "I knew her as Élodie Rousseau. I called her Ello. As did her parents."

Her parents were the missing friends who'd taught him French. Faith translated the news to Eagle.

"I thought she said Yellow when she was actually saying Ello." A muted chuckle rumbled in his chest. "After calling her one name for so long, it will be difficult to use another."

Faith leaned against him and held his gaze. "She will always be our Yellow Feather."

"And I will always be grateful that I found her and you." Eagle's hand tightened around hers. "I have always wondered something. Will you ask him...?"

"Yes. What is it you want to know?"

"Why has she never feared me?"

When Faith translated his question, Gray Owl traced the scar on his face. "Your scar probably reminds her of mine. She has always been fascinated by them because her parents turned wounds into scars. They were doctors. Unfortunately, some of my people believe a person who can heal an illness can also make the healthy sick. Good and evil, they are two sides of a face."

Dread constricted Faith's throat, but she made herself ask, "Have you any hope of finding her parents?"

Gray Owl's hand fell limply to his side. "One day, perhaps, I will find their bones."

Faith's heart ached for him and for the little girl, whom she'd yet to meet but already loved.

"I gave this spirit horse to the Rousseaus because

they saved my daughter's life. When I found the mare back in our tribe, with many trying to be her next rider, I suspected something unspeakable had happened. I was correct. No one would speak of what happened. So I wandered into the forest in search of the truth. All I discovered was a new friend bearing an image of him and my Ello. Now I find my new friend with you and surrounded by"—his gaze cut to their three attackers—"angry young Molalla men wishing to harm you. But you ride a sacred mount. You will be protected."

He looked at his warriors and said something in their language. They pulled the young men to the side of the trail, opening the path ahead.

When Gray Owl faced them again, his eyes were misty with unshed tears. "When you see your Yellow Feather, tell her that I miss my friends." He straightened his spine, and the determination of a chief blazed in his eyes. "Tell her I will see to it that she has safe passage over Molalla land. You will as well," he said, looking at Eagle. His gaze moved to Faith. "And so will—" Suddenly he laughed. "We have discussed many things, but not your name."

"It's Faith."

"I make this vow to you as well, Faith Feather. From this day forward, all three of you will be protected by Spirit and by me."

CHAPTER 8

*E*agle may have sat behind Faith, but he made no move to take the reins. She picked them up and urged Spirit forward along the trail. Eagle's horse followed close behind. When they reached the trail branch that Eagle had previously mentioned, the mare took the downhill path without any instruction.

The new route snaked down through the mist, dissipating as rapidly as the daylight. Faith's tension rose in opposite proportion to their descent.

"Do not worry," Eagle said. "We will arrive in a few minutes."

That's what worried her. As soon as they reached the end of this path, she'd have no reason to remain on Spirit or stay close to Eagle. The prospect constricted her chest and made it hard to breathe.

Eagle's arm circled her waist, holding her secure but also much too loosely. His body was as rigid as his tone when he said, "What's wrong?"

"Nothing's wrong."

"Then why are you shaking?"

"I'm just...tired." It had been a long day, but she didn't want it to end.

"Rest your head against my shoulder."

The panic squeezing her chest disappeared as soon as she did.

His sigh brushed the top of her head as he asked, "Where did you learn French?"

"A classmate at the academy taught me. My education was cut short when I had to leave for the logging camp."

"You speak it very well."

"Not compared to how well you speak English."

"My sister taught me."

"She did? How did she learn?"

"It is her first language. My mother adopted her when her parents were killed. She and Yellow Feather share that sorrow as well as the same yellow hair. I thought Blue Sky should be her mother."

"But she chose you." Slowly, inch by inch, her entire body relaxed against him, choosing him as well. "Earlier you said Yellow Feather added her name to yours. I never understood that. I'm also puzzled as to why Gray Owl called me Faith Feather. I never gave him my last name."

"Do you like the name?"

"I like it a lot."

"Would you be willing to share it with me forever?"

The thought of having a permanent connection to Eagle sparked her hope but did nothing to defuse her confusion. "Share how?"

"My name is Eagle Feather. That is why Gray Owl called you Faith Feather, and how Yellow Feather added her name to mine. Will you stay with me? I will do everything I can to be a good husband...if you would like to be my wife."

Her heart leapt with joy, but before she could reply, a woman's voice called, "Welcome home, Eagle Feather!"

A slender blonde woman waved from the doorway of a cabin in a clearing halfway down what remained of the path.

"That is my sister, Blue Sky. Her husband calls her Hannah."

The air smelled of recently hewn wood and sawdust. At the bottom of the slope, the path terminated beside a sawmill and a waterway. Her ride was over. She'd have to dismount from Spirit. Her stomach rolled with uncertainty.

What if the magic of this day ended as soon as she got off Spirit?

The girl from the daguerreotype, a miniature replica of Eagle's sister, ran out of the cabin and up the slope toward them. She'd found Yellow Feather, or rather Ello Rousseau. When the little girl stopped beside Spirit, her curious gaze inspected the mare and Faith as well. Then she made a series of rapid and unusual hand gestures.

"What's she doing?" Faith asked.

"She is speaking with her hands, asking where I found Spirit and you. When she would not talk, other than to tell me her name, I taught her my people's sign language." Eagle made several fluid hand signals in return.

Faith had no idea what they meant, but the look of adoration on the girl's face made Faith certain of one thing. "She's definitely your daughter."

He made more hand signals. "I am telling her your name and that I found you bringing Spirit back to her."

After he did, Yellow Feather made two more signs. Then she held up her hands in the universal signal of wanting to be picked up.

Eagle had to let go of Faith in order to reach down and lift the girl to sit on his hip. He kissed the top of her head. "I missed you too."

Faith twisted sideways on Spirit so she could see

them fully. Yellow Feather's small body snuggled into the curve of Eagle's arm.

She drew in a deep breath and chose her words carefully. *"Bonjour, Élodie. J'espère que nous pourrons être...amies."*

Yellow Feather stared at her without a sound or a gesture. Then she slowly shook her head.

Faith's shoulders slumped. *"Non?"*

Even though it made him wince, Eagle used his injured arm to hold her as well. "What did you say to her?"

"That I hoped we could be friends."

Yellow Feather's gaze went to Eagle's sister, who watched from the cabin doorway. The little girl drew in a breath as deep as Faith had done a moment ago, then said in a determined voice, "Auntie—teach—names." She patted Eagle's chest. "Papa." Her hand moved to Faith's. "Papa's wife." She nodded with certainty. *"Maman."*

Tears blurred Faith's eyes as she nodded as well. "You're right, of course. I'm marrying your father."

Yellow Feather's tiny hand grabbed Faith's arm. With a surprisingly strong grip, she pulled Faith closer to her and Eagle. "Ello Feather's family."

Over the top of her sweet golden head, Eagle smiled at Faith. "Our daughter has learned a lot in one day. So have I."

When Faith leaned her head toward him, he

bowed his until his brow found a home against her temple.

"You've learned we are strongest when we ride together?" She couldn't stop her smile and the impulse to coax one from him as well. "Which Spirit probably knew all along, so always listen to her?"

Eagle's soft laughter warmed her cheek, fortifying her body and spirit. "Yes. But also, always follow your heart. Your head will catch up soon enough."

Thanks for reading *Following Faith!*
If you enjoyed the story, see the next page to learn how posting a book review can make an author's day.

Craving more adventures in the Wild West?
Keep reading to see my story inspiration for *Following Faith* & an excerpt from *Choosing Bravery* (where Yellow Feather's adventure as an adult and a wilderness guide lead her to legendary Far North fugitive tracker, Lachlan Bravery) in Oregon's Cascade Mountains, 1868.

DEAR READER

I hope you enjoyed Faith and Eagle's story.

If you did, please consider posting a review online or email it to me at Jacqui@JacquiNelson.com

Every single review helps. No matter how long or short, they are a heartfelt gift that is sincerely appreciated. Hearing from readers makes my day and keeps me motivated to write my next book. Looking forward to hearing from you!

You can review *Following Faith* on Amazon, Goodreads, or BookBub. Or even all three.

AMAZON
amazon.com/author/jacquinelson

GOODREADS
goodreads.com/jacquinelson

BOOKBUB
bookbub.com/authors/jacqui-nelson

STORY INSPIRATION & NOTES

Following Faith came to life after I was asked to write a short story for the historical romance anthology *Journey of the Heart,* featuring forms of Old West transportation.

I'd always planned to give Hannah's brother, Eagle Feather (first seen in *Between Heaven & Hell*) his own story. Oregon became the setting since that was where Hannah had settled, and I wanted his path to reconnect with Hannah's.

Next came the decision of what transportation to use. Train, boat, stagecoach, wagon, or just plain old horseback—which I never find plain when every horse is unique. A childhood memory of a very unique horse and a much-loved book sprang to mind.

San Domingo, the Medicine Hat Stallion first published in 1972 by Marguerite Henry (with illustrations by Robert Lougheed) was re-published as *Peter Lundy and the Medicine Hat Stallion* in 1972 (when it became a TV movie). Set in Pony Express-era Wyoming, the story's core is the bond between a boy and a pinto horse with a very specific and rare color pattern—a mostly white body, neck, and head with a darker color that covers the top of the horse's head and ears like a bonnet or a hat.

Native legend said such a horse held the medicine to protect its rider from harm. The horse was greatly coveted and often stolen by those who wished to safeguard their—or a loved one's—life.

~ Jacqui

EXCERPT ~ CHOOSING BRAVERY
Lonesome Hearts Series

*When legends collide, will the sparks ignite their love or
drive them apart?*

After her parents vanished in the wilderness, Élodie
Rousseau found a home with an Osage warrior and
a logging camp schoolmistress who joined forces to
return Élodie's beloved spirit horse. With them as
her teachers, she became the legendary Cascade
Mountain guide, Yellow Feather. She knows
everything about surviving and thriving in the wild,
but something is missing.

Legendary Far North fugitive tracker, Lachlan Bravery,
is tortured by his failure to find the one person who
mattered most—the mentor who taught him
everything he once held sacred. Driven to repay a dead
man, his hunt for a notorious band of outlaws brings
him to Élodie's mountain, where they must join forces
on a final quest deep inside a cave with the power to
destroy not only their unexpected love but their lives.

Brave the wild. Bury the past.
Choose your destiny.

CHAPTER 1

Cascade Mountains, Oregon – 1868

The scent of fresh blood on an undercurrent of primeval decay choked Élodie Rousseau, nearly bringing her to her knees. She strove to keep her steps silent in the snow below the cave's gaping black maw. High above the evergreens stretching to the mountain peak, the midday sun blazed down. The pocket of white shone brutally bright but gave no warmth.

A cold sweat chilled her to the bone and played havoc with her grip on her rifle. The scream that sent her sprinting up the final leg of the ascent still rang in her ears, echoing with disbelief and horror.

Gray Owl was right. Only death lived in this once sacred place.

A wise daughter of the land would've heeded her old friend's warning to stay away, to look to the future, to focus on her gift of helping people find their way in the wilderness... rather than getting lost in the past. But death was what had drawn her to this isolated mountain cave.

Were her parents inside? After sixteen years,

would she finally find their remains only to stay with them forever?

The leather-skinned prospector she'd heard drowning his demons in Fort Shelton's rum-hole had babbled like a spooked greenhorn. This cavern, he'd proclaimed, contained far too many bones. The human kind. Lost loved ones lay here. Long forgotten.

Not so her parents. She'd never stopped searching for a glimpse of them in everyone she met.

Behind a jagged fall of rock, barely a dozen strides up the slope, the humped shoulders of a giant creature rose like a phantom.

She froze with her finger on her rifle's trigger. Her adoptive father, Eagle Feather's advice steadied her hand: *Never shoot until you see, with clear eyes, what you might kill.*

To read more about *Choosing Bravery*, visit
JacquiNelson.com

Be sure to add *Choosing Bravery* to your
"want to read" shelf on Goodreads at
Goodreads.com/jacquinelson

BETWEEN HEAVEN & HELL - EXCERPT
Lonesome Hearts Series, Book 1

On a trail full of danger,
will he guide her to heaven or hell?

Hannah knows one thing the moment she enters Fort Leavenworth—she's arrived in Hell. But inside is the means to a new life, a position as a scout on a wagon train bound for the Western Territories. All she has to do is convince the wagon master, Paden Callahan, she's the right person for the job.

After his wife was murdered by the Comanche, Paden let his work as a Texas Ranger consume him. Now he wants nothing more than to disappear into the West. Unfortunately, the one man he can't refuse has asked him to guide a wagon train full of tenderfoots across thousands of miles of Indian land. But Paden's greatest challenge turns out to be Hannah, a woman his heart won't allow him to ignore even though she was raised by an enemy he hates.

PROLOGUE
Kansas—1839

One minute the men were talking to her papa, the next they shot him dead.

Barely tall enough to see over the window sill, nine-year-old Hannah watched the tattered band of militiamen celebrate by riding circles around her family's cabin, whiskey bottles in one hand, roaring pistols in the other. Their whooping laughter conveyed the pleasure they took in taunting those left alive inside.

Terror kicked Hannah's legs out from under her, leaving her huddled on the dirt floor of her home. She clamped her hands over her ears, tried to shut out the gunshots, the pounding hooves, the jeers and calls for her and her mother to come outside.

But Mama did not heed them. Instead, she crouched beside Hannah and fired her own gun to keep their attackers at bay.

Suddenly, all sound ceased.

Mustering what little courage she had left, Hannah rose on trembling legs to once again peer out the window. The men had stopped circling. Had they grown bored of galloping around in the midday sun amid the clouds of churning dust?

Their sweat-streaked faces were lowered as they

stuffed scraps of cloth down the necks of their whiskey bottles. Had they grown tired of drinking, too?

Bright orange flames burst from the bottle tops. Putting heel to horse, the renegade mob rushed the cabin. Hannah jerked back in disbelief. The men tossed their makeshift torches onto the roof and then withdrew to a safe distance, knowing she and her mother were still inside. Mama's rifle had told them so.

Dreading what she might see, Hannah's gaze rose to the ceiling. A slash of red ripped across the wood planks, then another and another, like the eyes of a dozen demons. With a shriek, she flung herself into her mother's outstretched arms. The cabin crackled and hissed. The flames snaked all around her, making her skin hurt like she'd come too near a boiling pot.

A shroud of charcoal covered the sunbeams in her mother's hair, and her voice was hoarse with the same ash that choked Hannah's lungs when she spoke. "Climb out the back window. Run faster than you've ever run. Head for the ravine. Hide under its brambles."

Hannah nodded. Mama always knew what to do. She would save them.

Her mother's cornflower-blue eyes glistened. Her

gaze slid slowly over Hannah's face as if memorizing it. Then she blinked, and her gaze locked on the window. "I'll keep firing. They won't know you've left. They won't come after you if they think we're still inside."

Hannah hesitated.

"Go on now." Mama's push was gentle, but her tone had turned firm. "I'll come as soon as I can."

Reluctantly, Hannah obeyed. She ran until her lungs ached. When she reached the bramble bushes a hundred yards away, she ignored the thorns that tore her clothing and cut her skin. She crawled under the tangle of twigs until she could go no farther. Lying on her belly with her cheek pressed against the hard earth, she listened to the comforting crack of her mother's rifle.

Soon she'd come out and join her...wouldn't she?

Uncertainty pinned Hannah down. So did the brambles above her. She couldn't breathe. She had to get out. With a gasp, she clawed the dirt, trying to scramble back the way she'd come. Her home burst into a roaring ball of fire. *Mama! You have to come out!*

The cabin buckled in on itself and collapsed.

Clutching her knees to her chest, Hannah let her tears burn her cheeks. The militiamen's yelling faded as they left. They left her with no reason to move or live. She stayed under the brambles and gave in to the sweet oblivion darkening the corners of her vision.

The pounding of hooves startled her awake. She squinted through the twigs. The towering funnel cloud of black smoke had faded to a wisp of a memory. A band of raven-haired riders halted between her and the charred remains of her home. Even though she was embedded deep in her hiding place, one of them turned in her direction. And pointed.

They were Indians! Fear constricted her throat. White men had shot Papa and burned Mama alive. What would these people, who everyone called savages, do to her?

They dug her out. When they reached her, she screamed and fought like an animal. The men drew back as if bewildered by such fierceness in one so small. They didn't go far, though. They formed a circle around her. Dark statues with sharp-cut features, they uttered not a word as the lines of their faces settled into impenetrable granite.

Their silence unnerved her as much as the white militiamen's noise. She darted around her cage, seeking an escape. She found none. Gasping for air, she fell to her knees.

A woman pushed through the wall of bodies holding her captive. Hannah tensed, wanting again to flee. But her legs wouldn't obey. All she could do was stare through stinging eyes.

Tall and straight as any queen, the woman wore no jewels or garments of grandeur. Her mane of glossy black hair was her crown, her simple buck-skin dress her mantle. She didn't watch Hannah with the curiosity of a stranger or the calculating look of a superior. Instead, her dark eyes glistened with compassion...with understanding.

Surrounded by a ring of emotionless faces and the stench of her smoldering home, the smallest ember of hope flickered inside Hannah. Acting on instinct, she raced forward, throwing herself into the woman's arms—and into a whole new world.

CHAPTER 1

11 years later...
Fort Leavenworth, Kansas—Spring 1850

Lord help her, for she had entered Hell. That Hannah had sought guidance from the God of her past made her loneliness increase tenfold. She should've prayed to Grandfather Spider.

"Well, what'a we got here?" someone yelled from behind her. The voice was rough with malicious undertones.

"Don't reckon I know," replied another man. "Though she be a purty lil' yellow-haired thing."

"Maybe, but we'd hafta get them injun' clothes off her to tell fer sure."

Hannah stiffened in her saddle but kept her buckskin-clad knees tight against White Cloud's sides, urging him forward. She fought the need to tug down the frayed cuffs of her wool coat or touch the beads and feathers on her belt for comfort.

Don't react, she told herself. *Don't make eye contact. Don't turn back.*

A mountain man, the size of a bear, spat a foul-smelling stream of brown chewing tobacco in front of White Cloud's path. He sneered at Hannah with lips stretched over rotting teeth.

Behind him on a saloon porch, a trio of dusty cowhands rose from their card game, waved their whiskey bottles at her and hollered, "Ooh-wee, lovey! Come on down from yer horse. Let us show you a good time."

Strident feminine laughter filled the air. Hannah's gaze darted heavenward to discover a row of women dressed in corsets and short calico skirts. They leaned over the balcony railing, watching her with black-rimmed eyes full of disdain.

If she ignored them, maybe they'd leave her alone. Or maybe coming to Fort Leavenworth hadn't been such a good idea. She had no choice. She couldn't turn back.

To read more about *Between Heaven & Hell*, visit JacquiNelson.com

Don't forget to add *Between Heaven & Hell* to your "want to read" shelf on Goodreads at Goodreads.com/jacquinelson

PRAISE FOR THE LONESOME HEARTS SERIES...

Between Heaven & Hell

"A perfect, steady-paced book with poetic descriptions of romance and easy-to-follow fluidity of Callahan and Hannah's journeys." ~ Chanticleer Book Reviews

"A fire-cracker of a love story with the perfect blend of fascinating characters, intense emotion, historical drama and fast-paced action." ~ Scarlett Penn

"Beautiful writing and flawed characters it was easy to care about. A thoroughly engaging story I enjoyed tremendously." ~ Lark

"An exciting journey filled with perilous adventure, this is an original interesting tale with a woven plot line that comes full circle." ~ InD'tale Magazine

Following Faith

"The first story I'd read by Jacqui Nelson which put her on my watch-out-for-and-read-her-stuff list. Despite the short length, this story packed a big punch." ~ Michelle R.

"So well written and so descriptive, you easily get transported to the old west and are traveling on the trail with Faith and Eagle. A beautiful, sweet, romantic, heartwarming story you won't want to miss." ~ Barb

Jacqui Nelson "has a unique way of drawing the reader back to the old west with colorful descriptions and characters who leap from the page." ~ Jacquie B.

Choosing Bravery

"Grand adventure. Mystery and excitement." ~ Sandra S.

"Action packed, fabulous setting and two main characters you could really root for" ~ N. Love

"One of those stories that just takes you away to a world of the wild west, filled with adventure, suspense and sweet romance. I couldn't put it down." ~ B

Rescuing Raven - free for my newsletter subscribers

"Grabbed my interest from the first page and did not let go until the end." ~ Babs

"Beautifully written...Don't pass this short story by. You will not be disappointed." ~ Sandy S.

"I loved this short story and you will too." ~ Dorothy R.

WANT A FREE E-BOOK?

Sign up for my newsletter at JacquiNelson.com
and download for free *Rescuing Raven*
(a standalone story but also part of my *Lonesome Hearts* series, which can be read in any order).

Deadwood, Dakota Territory 1876...
In a gold rush storm, can an unlikely pair rescue each other?
Raven wants to save one person. Charlie wants to save the world. Their warring nations thrust them together but duty pulled them apart—until their paths crossed again in Deadwood for a fight for love.

EXCERPT
RESCUING RAVEN - CHAPTER 1

Fighting a growing impatience fueled by rage, Charlie Jennings drew his revolver and urged his horse through the trees flanking the Deadwood Trail. Below him, an Appaloosa with the strikingly similar color of his own horse—white covered from head to hock in chestnut spots—was rein-tied to the back of a buckboard. If the horse hadn't caught his attention, he might not have given the transport a second look.

He might not have seen her.

The wagon rattled forward carrying one silent and seven grumbling passengers. When a bend in the trail cast the sun in the eyes of the guards, one riding behind and the other in front, he charged his spotted mare down onto the road.

Everyone in the wagon, except for the cowering raven-haired woman, screamed. The driver jerked on the lines. The horses skidded to a halt. The guards scrambled for their weapons.

The click of his revolver being cocked made them all freeze.

The silence that followed was as heated as the summer sun on his back. The guards glared at him through squinted eyes. He kept his focus on them as well—lined up in a neat row down the barrel of his Colt Peacemaker.

"Jennings," growled the closest man, who went by the name Big Bill. "You shouldn't be here."

"Yeah," hollered Bill's partner, a stranger who resembled a beanpole.

Frontier trails and towns had a way of attracting similarly named men, including the Charlies like him. They also had a fondness for embellishment. The deck was stacked in favor of the rear guard being called Skinny Sam or Loudmouth Pete.

"We heard you were guidin' a miner 'n his four kids, the ones who lost their ma, away from Deadwood." At least Skinny hadn't heard, and used, the double-barreled moniker Charlie had been saddled with since arriving in the Black Hills.

"But you," he shot back, "didn't hear that my job finished ahead of schedule."

"Well," Bill said on a long breath, "ain't that a spot of bad luck."

"Not for one of your passengers." He didn't look her way. He'd already seen enough: a ragtag assortment of women, one hunched with her dark head over her wrists tied to the wagon.

To read the rest of *Rescuing Raven*, visit my website JacquiNelson.com and sign up for my newsletter.

Rescuing Raven - Deadwood, 1876, a FREE read for

my newsletter subscribers

≈

GAMBLING HEART SERIES

Between Love & Lies - Book 1, Dodge City, 1877

Between Home & Heartbreak - Book 2, Texas, 1879

≈

STEAM! ROMANCE AND RAILS

Adella's Enemy - Kansas, 1870

≈

To learn more about my books, visit my website

JacquiNelson.com

ABOUT THE AUTHOR

Fall in love with a new Old West... where the men are steadfast and the women are adventurous. You'll find Wild West scouts, spies, cardsharps, wilderness guides, and trick-riding superstars in my stories. Those are my heroines. Wait till you meet my heroes!

My love for historical romance adventures with grit and passion came from watching Western movies while growing up on a cattle farm in northern Canada. I've been nominated for over 20 awards and won the RWA® Golden Heart® & the Laramie® — but my best reward is hearing from readers who have enjoyed my stories.

Email me at Jacqui@JacquiNelson.com

For updates on giveaways, special events, and more, join my newsletter at JacquiNelson.com amazon.com/Jacqui-Nelson/e/B00EE6GE88

goodreads.com/JacquiNelson

bookbub.com/authors/jacqui-nelson

facebook.com/JacquiNelsonAuthor

instagram.com/jacquinelsonauthor

pinterest.com/JacquiAuthor

x.com/Jacqui_Nelson

youtube.com/@jacquinelsonauthor

tiktok.com/@jacquinelsonauthor